Hot Rod Hamster

MEETS HIS MATCH!

By **Cynthia Lord**

Cover illustration by **Derek Anderson**

Interior illustrations by **Greg Paprocki**

Scholastic Press • New York

To my Hot Rod Hamster match, Derek Anderson — C. L.

For my grandparents, Marvin and Lyda Anderson — D. A.

Text copyright © 2016 by Cynthia Lord
Illustrations copyright © 2016 by Derek Anderson

Library of Congress Cataloging-in-Publication Data available

ISBN 978-0-545-82592-4

10 9 8 7 6 5 4 3 2 1   16 17 18 19 20

Printed in Malaysia   108
First edition, February 2016

The display type was set in Ziggy ITC and Coop Black.
The text was set in Cochin Medium and Gill Sans Bold.
The interior art was created digitally by Greg Paprocki.
Art direction and book design by Marijka Kostiw

It was a hot summer day. Hot Rod Hamster and his friends wanted to feel cool, so they went to a place with a pool.

Let's have some cool, wet, and wild fun!
An ice pop will cool us off.

Grape pop. Punch pop. Fudge pop. Crunch pop.

Which would *you* choose?

Round float.   Square float.

Shark float.   Chair float.
Which would *you* choose?

Dog sips his drink. Hamster gives a sigh.
Mice point to show a waterslide up high.

That waterslide looks too wild for me! We'll watch you come down.
Okay. Look for the fastest tube and the biggest splash! That'll be me.

Striped tube.   Bright tube.

Race tube.   White tube.
Which would *you* choose?

We need more speed!
If we lie down, air will flow past us more easily. We'll go faster.

Dog gives a gasp as the racers round the bend.
Mice are surprised to see . . .

Hot Rod Hamster and a friend.